BY THE STREAM

A Nature Story

by Lilian McCrea and Michael Twinn

Illustrated by Richard Hook

Models by Brian Edwards

Rand McNally

Published in the US.A. by Rand McNally & Company.
First published in England by Wm. Collins Sons & Co. Ltd. 1972
Bound and printed in Milan, Italy
Text copyright © Key Facts (UK) Limited and Lilian McCrea 1972
Illustrations Copyright © Key Facts (UK) Limited 1972
ISBN   528-82677-8

SPRING had come to the woodlands and the Stream rejoiced. Her banks were radiant with flowers — bluebells, forget-me-nots, anemones, violets and golden celandines. Mayflies danced above her shining water, trout jumped and splashed, tiny fishes darted in and out among the water weeds. On a stone, still as a statue, sat the Frog.

It was evening and the moon showed her pale face above the trees.

"Are you asleep, Frog?" asked the Stream. In reply, out shot his sticky tongue and scooped up an unsuspecting fly. The Stream rippled with laughter.

"You are so patient," she said.

"You have to be to catch flies," croaked the Frog dryly. "We've been catching flies for centuries."

"I know," admonished the Stream. "I was there when you were still learning."

"Don't be so tiresome," croaked the Frog. "You don't know everything."

THEY were quite good friends really, but the Stream resented the Frog's independence, for he would often leave her banks and not be seen for weeks. Before she could reply, a bird dipped and skimmed over her waters. It was a Hawk. High in a tree, far out in the wood, he had a

nest of hungry fledglings. A Frog would satisfy their hunger!

"Kek, kek, kek!"

The Hawk dropped like a stone. Splash! The Frog dived into the water and disappeared. He was safe!

"Very good," said the Stream. "Very good, you are improving."

The Frog emerged and resumed his sentinel position. "Why didn't you warn me?" he said.

"I didn't warn the fly, did I?" replied the Stream. "You know I never take sides. If I took sides, it would change the course of history." The Stream pursued her favorite theme. "*They* take sides, the Men I mean, and look at the result."

"They've changed your course, haven't they?", replied the Frog with a husky laugh. "But you're quite right, they've made life very difficult for all of us."

THE conversation was disturbed by a snuffling and grunting on the bank. The Frog prepared to jump again.

"Calm down," said the Stream. "It's only a Hedgehog. He doesn't like to come too near the water." Together they watched him nosing his way along, grunting his satisfaction as he came upon a fat slug or beetle.

The Hedgehog sniffed the air. The breeze was

bringing a strange scent. Ah! There it was, lying under a bramble bush looking like a twisted stick. An Adder! The Hedgehog stopped in his tracks. Slightly, the Snake uncoiled and raised its head. Its eyes glittered. Its tongue darted in and out. The Hedgehog was not afraid. Suddenly he rushed at the Snake, pulling his front spines down over his face.

With an angry hiss, the Snake struck and recoiled as it felt the sharp pricks of the Hedgehog's bristles. For less than a second, the Hedgehog uncovered his head. Before the Snake could recover, he seized it by the tail and coiled himself into a ball. Again and again the Snake struck and

again and again it recoiled in pain. But the Hedgehog never relaxed his hold until, at last, he felt the Snake grow limp.

"How brave he is," said the Frog, who was terrified of Adders.

The Hedgehog overheard.

"It was nothing," he sniffed, pausing from his meal. "We have been catching snakes for millions of years. Our spines protect us from practically anything."

"Have you tried them against Men?" interrupted the Stream.

"There's no need," replied the Hedgehog. "Men like us. . . . If only they wouldn't drive so

fast in those infernal cars of theirs. At night, they fix us in the glare of their headlights, and nothing can save us if we are directly in their path. It is much more dangerous than falling in water."

"MMM," murmured the Stream, moving uncomfortably and sending a shower of spray over some pebbles on the bank. One of the pebbles moved. It was a Snail. He poked out his little head.

"It isn't the Stream's fault if you don't swim very well. Why, I wish I had spines instead of this flimsy shell. Blackbirds crack it open in a second and even if I see them coming I can't move fast enough."

"Now, now," consoled the Stream. "Your shell is a perfect disguise."

"That's true," admitted the Snail. "And it's very beautiful. Of course, we've had millions of years to develop it." Then he continued sadly. "But now it's not just Blackbirds we have to worry about. The Men persecute us because we eat their plants. They are very cruel." The timid Snail drew back into the protection of the long grass. The Hedgehog returned to his nest. Only the Frog lingered to keep the Stream company.

Two Thrushes came down to the Stream and paddled in her shallows. They splashed the bright drops around and preened their feathers. A Squirrel leaped nimbly from the bank to a stone at the water's edge. He drank deeply, then smoothed his bushy tail and leaped back into the woodlands.

THEN came a Pheasant, resplendent in bronze and green and crimson. He sipped the cool water and stood gazing in admiration at his own reflection.

In the undergrowth, a short distance away, someone else was admiring the lordly bird. It was the Fox, the Red Hunter of the woodlands.

Stealthily, the Fox, crept nearer, nearer. The Stream shuddered.

"Kut! Kut! Kut!" A Squirrel barked a warning.

With a rush and a scurry, the Pheasant leaped into the air. The Fox sprang. Snap! For once, he was too late. All that he was left with was a single golden feather.

Dusk deepened into darkness. Lazily, the Stream flowed, waiting and listening. Suddenly, a high whistle sounded over the water. "Now there'll be some fun," she told the Frog. "Watch!"

AN Otter swam out from the shallows. He clambered onto the bank and sniffed the air. When he was sure there was no danger, he plunged into the water again and swam towards the den where his mate and young ones waited. He whistled

again, "All is safe."

His mate came first, diving from the den into the water. "Come on!" she whistled, and three young Otters, too nervous yet to dive, scrambled and slid down the bank and swam towards her.

The whole family was in the water now. They rolled and ducked and floated. Father Otter rolled himself into a ball and burst open with a loud splash when the others tried to catch him. Then, one after another, they swam towards the bank and climbed out of the water, their wet coats gleaming in the moonlight. For a moment, they stood sniffing the air. All was safe for their favorite game.

Back into the water they dived and swam towards a deep pool. Once there, they raced to the top of the steep bank and slid down into the water. Splash! Splash! Splash! Again and again. The Stream gurgled with laughter. Round and round they went in the moonlight, round and round.

A twig snapped. Instantly, the Otters disappeared into the water. "That's enough for tonight," said Father Otter. "We can't take any risks." But before returning to the den he caught a fine fat trout.

THE moon climbed high in the sky. Now its light was so bright that the Stream could see the leaves of the willows shining like silver. An Owl flew over the trees, his ghostly call quavering off into the stillness, "Whoo . . . whoo . . . whoo . . . whoo!" A Weasel, long and slender, flashed through the ferns, following the trail. A Nighthawk swooped among the moths that darted in the moonbeams. Silently, a Bat flew homewards. Soon, the night was still. The winged creatures were asleep and the hunters had returned to their holes. The Stream flowed on, dreaming of the day that was to come.

At last, dawn came peeping. The birds burst into their joyful chorus and soon the woodlands were flushed with the light of the morning sun. A young Hare pirouetted in the grass. A Squirrel raced up an oak tree and, flattening himself along the branch, peeped down mischievously.

Early on the scene was the Fox. His disappointment with the Pheasant was forgotten. In the meantime he had stolen a Chicken and now he was in search of further prey.

IN the Stream, beneath the elm tree, on a platform of twigs and rushes she had made, a little brown Water Vole was sitting, cleaning her soft fur. Suddenly she was startled by a stranger to

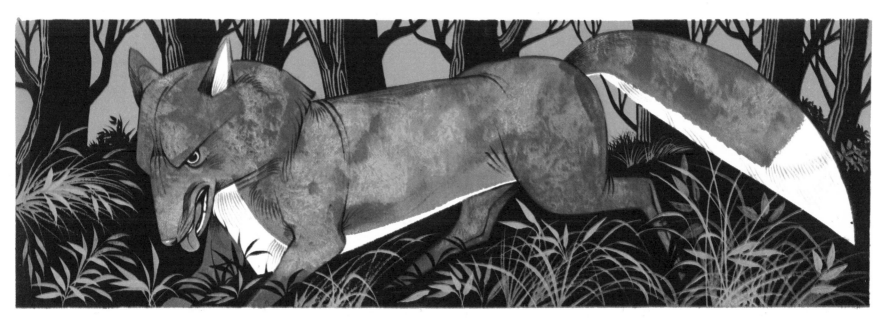

the woodland. It was a Tortoise. He crawled along, enjoying the walk in the sun, pausing to nibble a young leaf of dandelion. The Stream watched him with great interest.

"Come over here," she beckoned softly. "There are masses of buttercups on my banks. It's a million years since I saw anyone like you around here."

"I'm not from here," said the Tortoise. "Some Men brought me thousands of miles from my homeland."

"What interference!" said the Stream. "Why, it's not warm enough for you here."

"Oh, it's all right," replied the Tortoise.

"Actually, they were very kind. I lived for many years in a garden. Children fed me and protected me from danger, and in the Fall when the winds blew chill, they put me to rest in a bed of clean straw."

"Then why are you here?" asked the Frog.

"One day last summer," continued the Tortoise with a sad smile, "I wandered out of the garden and lost my way. I spent the winter in a bed of leaves, in a hollow tree trunk."

As the Tortoise talked, he stretched out his neck towards the buttercups close to the water's edge. Suddenly he lost his balance, fell over the edge of the bank, landed on the pebbles below and

overturned. He was helpless. He lay there, his little legs feebly clawing the air.

"If somebody does not rescue me," he gasped, "I will surely die."

"I'm sorry," said the Stream, "There is nothing I can do."

"Don't worry," croaked the Frog. "Humans can't be far away."

A Boy and a Girl came running and leaping down to the Stream. "Isn't it lovely," they cried as they looked at the banks radiant with flowers and the willows wafting their green wands. Soon the Girl had collected a large bouquet.

They watched the Trout jumping and splash-ing and the tiny fish darting in and out among the water weeds. "I wish I had my fishing rod," said the Boy. Then he saw one of the Frog's sisters. "Is she asleep?" asked the Girl.

"No," said the Boy. "Watch!" And suddenly, out shot the sticky tongue to scoop up an un-suspecting fly. Then the Boy threw a stone. He did not know why, it was probably just to make the Frog hop. How the children laughed to see her dive into the safety of the water.

DEEP in the grass, they spied the Snail. He was clinging to a rock sheltered by the fronds of the ferns. "He thinks he's safe," laughed the

Boy. "Shall I kill him? Daddy says that Snails are pests."

"No," exclaimed the Girl. "His shell is so beautiful and he is doing no harm here."

The Boy thought for a moment, then his gaze was attracted by something new. He had seen the path where the grass was crushed by the Hedgehog's spines and under a bramble bush, they found the signs of his fearful fight with the Adder. "Look," said the Boy. "There's the remains of a dead snake. I wonder what killed it!"

Then they found a Pheasant's feather and a little further on they surprised the lordly bird himself. Up from a low-lying bush he sprang and with whirring wings soared away through the trees, a streak of green and bronze and crimson. "Isn't it beautiful?" said the little Girl. "I wonder if there are any eggs to collect?" said the Boy.

Now they reached a dark pool. "Shh!" said the Boy. "I thought I saw something." The smooth shadows parted and a wet, shining head appeared. It was the Otter. He rolled and floated, looped the loop, and swam on his back and on his side. The children laughed and the Otter disappeared from sight.

"LET'S look over there," said the Boy. They came to the elm tree where, in a sheltered hole under the roots, the Water Vole had her nest. They lay on the grass and peered over the bank. They saw the pebbles gleaming white at the water's edge . . . Then they saw the Tortoise lying on his back. "Look! Look! Look!" they cried. "It's our Tortoise." They jumped down among the pebbles and picked him up.

"Is he dead?" asked the Girl.

"No," said the Boy. "He's moving his head." They put him down in the grass near the tree in which the Hedgehog was sleeping. Slowly but surely, the little creature put out his head and feebly moved it from side to side.

JOYFULLY, the children bore the Tortoise away. In the silence left behind them, the Stream returned to her favorite theme. As always, she found a willing listener in Frog.

"Thank heaven, they have gone," complained the Stream. "Nasty, noisy creatures. Disturbing the balance of nature."

"Well, I make it about fifty-fifty," croaked the Frog solemnly. "They are unpredictable all right, and they think they own the place. But just think what they could do if they make the right choice."

"I wish I had your patience Frog," said the Stream. "Let's hope they'll learn."

Hints on Folding

Separate the six Origami sheets from the book by carefully cutting along the left hand edge of each model.

Always fold on a flat, smooth and hard surface.

Make the folds as carefully as possible along the folding lines. Heavy black folding lines (- - - - - - - -) are always on the *INSIDE* of the fold. Sometimes a thin dotted line (.........) shows where to make a fold and this may be on the outside.

Lightly press the fold, then check that it follows the folding line before pressing it down firmly with your fingernail.

As you make a fold, keep an eye on the drawing that follows it to make sure that each stage is right before starting the next one.

Each stage is numbered. Read the whole of a stage and be sure that you understand it before you make the fold on your model.

On pages 16 and 17 you will find a background so that you can act out the story with your completed models. Just prop the book upright. We suggest the models are made in the following order: Frog, Tortoise, Hedgehog, Snail, Pheasant and Otter.

Now here is a simple test

1. Take a square piece of paper and fold it in half.
2. Fold it again at an angle.
3. Straighten it out again and make the same fold to the other side of the paper.
4. Straighten this out and make another fold at a slightly different angle further along the paper. Straighten it out and make the same fold to the other side of the paper as you did before.
5. Straighten this fold out and hold the top corners with each hand.
6. Open the paper out slightly and take the left corner down under the right one, as far as the second fold will allow.
7. Pull it forward again as far as the other fold will allow.
   This is the most difficult type of fold you will have to make with your Origami models.

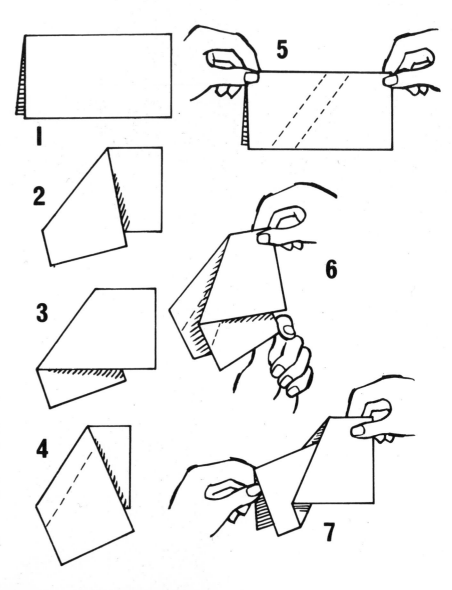

18

Tortoise

Here is an animal who wears its skeleton outside its skin, a living fossil that has changed little in the millions of years since dinosaurs ruled the Earth. In those remote times, their bodies were protected by horny plates. As time passed, the plates grew larger and closer together until they finally joined. Beneath the shell, skin and muscle wasted away until the shell rested on the bone. As evolution continued, these bones eventually attached themselves to the shell. In the modern tortoise, only hip bones and shoulder bones can still move within the shell.

In Ancient Egypt, Sheta the tortoise was a sacred animal. The ancient Greeks associated it with the goddess Aphrodite and depicted it on the face of some of their coins. The Roman method of locking shields together as a protection

19

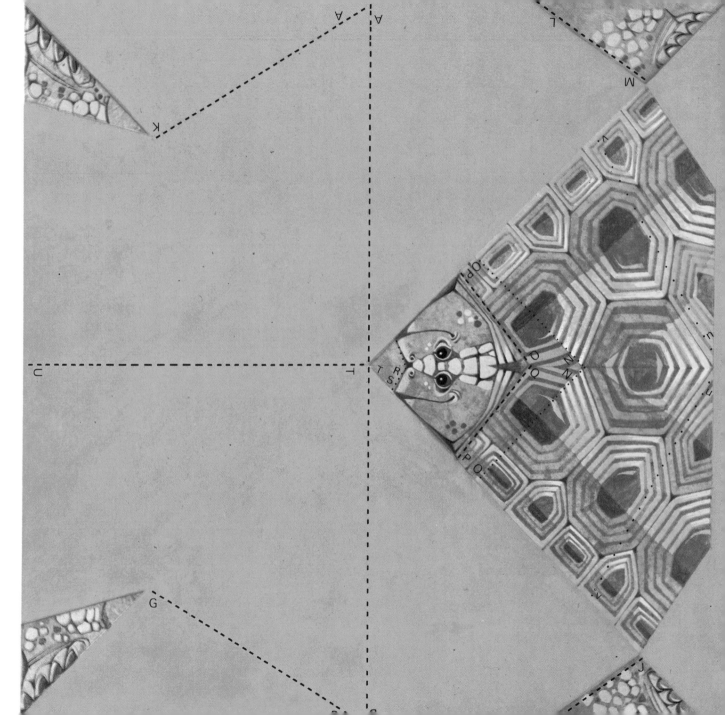

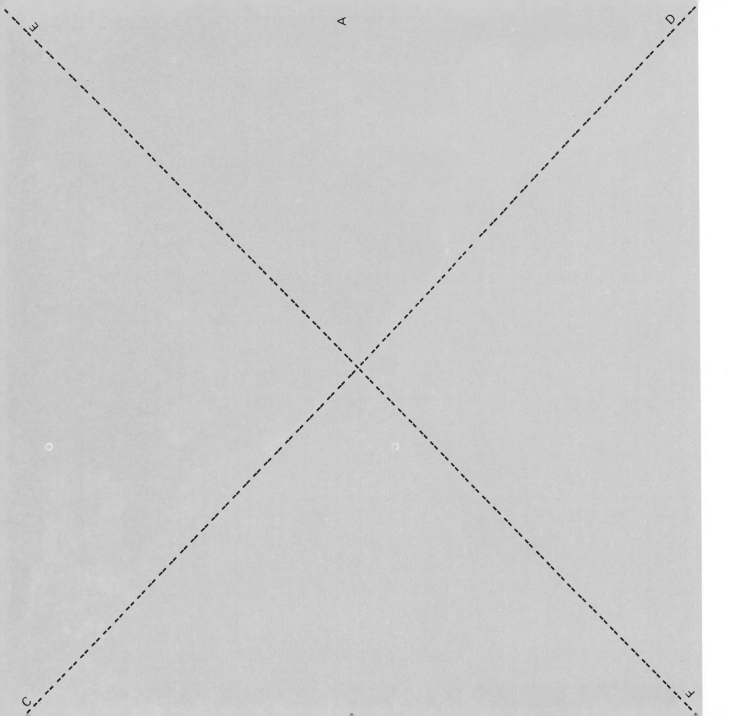

from missiles thrown down from a city wall was called the *testudo,* the Latin word for tortoise. Many ancient peoples have used the empty shell as a sound-box for stringed instruments. Throughout the ages, tortoiseshell has been used in many fine decorated objects.

In the 17th century, the great sea-going explorers discovered giant tortoises on the islands of the Indian and Pacific Oceans. They also discovered that they were good to eat. Untold thousands were loaded aboard ships to provide food on long voyages. These huge and ancient creatures almost became extinct, until in modern times they were protected by law and raised on farms, where their numbers are slowly increasing.

In 1773, Captain Cook, the great explorer of New Zealand, gave a giant tortoise of the species *testudo radiata* to the King of Tonga. It was highly prized and given the name Tu'imalila or King of Malila. It survived two forest fires, being run over by a cart and kicked by a horse. When it died on May 19, 1966, it must have been over 200 years old, the longest living creature on record.

Folding instructions are on page 31.

Otter

Here is a playful creature found in many parts of the world. It can climb and, for short distances, run as fast as a fox. Its webbed feet and thick, oily coat make it an accomplished underwater swimmer. Otters eat all kinds of fish, shellfish and eels. When these foods are not available, they live on small rodents, water-birds, frogs and worms.

There is no definite breeding season, cubs having been found in every month of the year, but mid-winter to May is the usual time for a litter of two or three to be born. The female makes a nest in a hollow in a river bank, or in hollow trees, between rocks, among reeds, or even among dead branches far from water. Both parents feed the cubs, bringing fish to the nest, until they are old enough to catch them for themselves. The dog otter then

21

leaves the family, the female remaining for most of the first year, teaching her cubs to hunt. Otter cubs are very playful and noisy, their cries often being heard at night.

The nocturnal habits of otters appear to have been acquired, rather than being natural. Otter hunting has made them wary of Man, but in remote areas they will hunt and fish as much in the daytime as at night. Yet they are friendly animals, easily tamed, and become very attached to humans who keep them as pets.

Out of the breeding season, otters will travel great distances. They seem to be occasionally attracted to salt-water, and can be found along the sea coasts and in estuaries where they live on rock fish and shellfish. There is a near-relation of the otter living along the shores of the North Pacific, particularly near the Aleutian Islands and Alaska. The sea-otter, as it is called, is highly unusual among animals in that it has learned to use a tool. It will hold two rocks in its forefeet and crush a shellfish between them, or balance the shellfish on its tummy while it floats on its back and cracks the shell with a single stone.

Folding instructions are on page 32.

22

Pheasant

This is the male bird with his white collar and dark green head, scarlet wattle and copper-colored plumage. The female is nothing like so splendid. She has soft brown plumage mottled with black and a shorter tail. The introduction of different varieties into game reserves has, however, resulted in differences of plumage in both sexes.

It is characteristic of pheasants that they walk about a good deal and can run very fast. When they do take to the air, they can startle you by rising almost vertically before you have spotted them in the long grass.

In the Spring, the males make a lot of noise, crowing and standing very upright while beating their wings. They spar with each other, standing face to face with their rump feathers raised and their tails

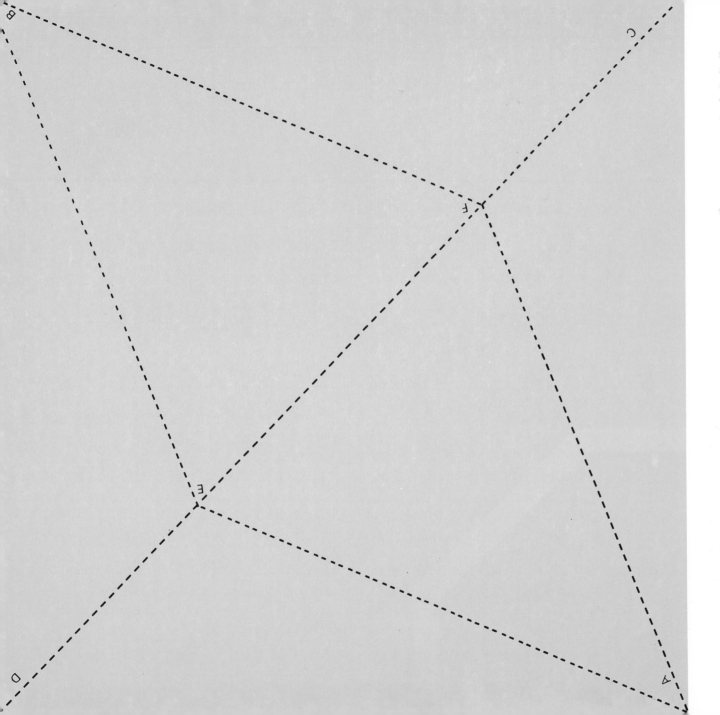

spread. They move their heads up and down in unison, until one suddenly pecks at the other, which is usually the signal for both to leap off the ground.

Having chosen his mate, the male struts round the female with puffed-out feathers and the wing nearest her spread out. The female scrapes out a hollow in the ground and lines it with a scattering of leaves and grass. Sometimes nests can be in haystacks, trees or even on a wall.

There are usually 8 to 15 olive-brown eggs which take three and a half weeks to incubate. More often, the female hatches the brood, though males have been recorded on the nest. The young leave the nest very shortly after hatching and are tended by the mother. They learn to fly after about two weeks, though their long tail feathers do not develop until the Fall. The young fledglings are a similar color to the mother bird.

Nests are not easy to find, though the mother can be watched returning to incubate her clutch of eggs. In most countries, the pheasant is a protected game bird and searching for their nests is frowned upon.

Folding instructions are on page 33.

Snail

This is a name given to various air-breathing gastropod, shelled mollusks. The word "gastropod" comes from the Greek words *gaster* meaning stomach and *pous* meaning foot. Snails do indeed have a single muscular foot, on which they slither about, attached to the stomach. Mollusks are animals without a backbone and with a soft body, also including such creatures as slugs, mussels and cuttlefish.

Snails are divided into two main families. The first has two tentacles that cannot be retracted into the head, with an eye at the base of each tentacle. The second family has two pairs of tentacles that can be retracted, with the eyes in the tips of the upper pair.

Snails feed almost entirely on vegetable matter. They have cut-

ters in the upper jaw, and a rasping ribbon in the mouth. Snails can be distinctively male or female, though many are both sexes at once. In this latter case, it is still necessary for one snail to fertilize the eggs of another.

The biggest snail of all is a sea snail called the Sea Hare which is found in coastal waters off California. They weigh an average seven or eight pounds, but there are records of specimens up to 16 pounds. The largest land snail is the African Giant Snail which can reach 10 inches in length and a pound in weight. Though it originated in Africa, it has been recently discovered in America. It was introduced into California among equipment salvaged from the Pacific area during the Second World War.

The Roman snail, *helix pomatia*, is the edible variety considered a great delicacy in France.

At the University of Maryland tests were carried out on the speed at which common garden snails can move. It was found that a snail's pace can be as slow as 0.00036 miles per hour or 23 inches in an hour. But it can speed up to 0.0313 miles per hour or a galloping 55 yards in an hour.

Folding instructions are on pages 34 & 35.

Hedgehog

This animal belongs to the large group called Insectivores or insect-eaters. Hedgehogs are rather primitive animals and have descended from the earliest small mammals of the Cretaceous period 120 million years ago. Even today, they are of low intelligence and slow-moving. They are covered in spines that grow up to an inch in length, and protect themselves by rolling into a ball and presenting an overall spiky surface to their enemies. Only badgers and foxes have found out how to unroll a hedgehog to get at the soft underbelly. Unfortunately, this means of defense is useless when a hedgehog finds itself in the path of an oncoming car. Hedgehogs that have been run over are a common sight on the country roads.

Yet hedgehogs are immune to a number of poisons. As well as

27

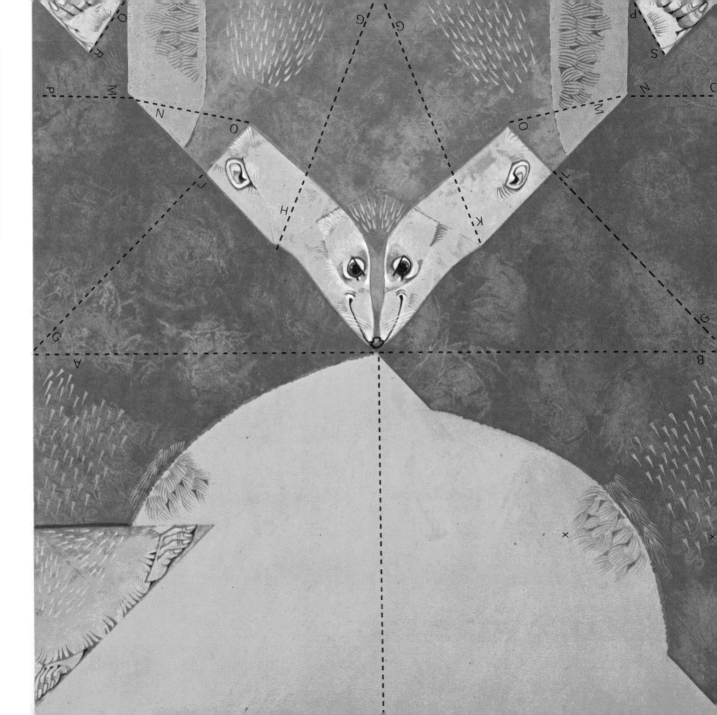

harmless insects, larvae, worms and snails, they can eat decaying flesh, wasps and even vipers. Because of this and their high rate of breeding, they are very numerous, even in built-up areas. They tend to hide in hedges, thickets and woodland during the day, only emerging in search of food at night. Their eyesight is poor, but their sense of smell is acute, and they can climb walls and fences.

The hibernation of hedgehogs seems to be a matter of temperature. If they are kept as pets in warm and well-fed conditions, they will remain active all Winter. They can even be roused from their Winter sleep if the temperature is raised. They have often been kept in gardens to keep down the slugs and other vermin. They have no fear of humans, and will soon learn to come into a garden at regular times each day for kitchen scraps and bread and milk set out for them.

The young are usually born in the Spring, though litters of four to six can be produced up to late Autumn. The babies are born blind, but already have their spikes. These become harder as the young grow rapidly and their eyes open.

Folding instructions are on page 36.

Frog

There are many varieties of frogs throughout the world. This is the common European marsh frog. Frogs, like toads, newts and salamanders, are amphibians which means they spend part of their life in water and part on dry land. Newts and salamanders have tails; frogs and toads do not. Amphibians are probably descended from the earliest lung fish who had swim-bladders connected with the throat so that they could breathe air, and were the first living creatures to crawl on to dry land.

The female frog lays her eggs in shallow water, and they are fertilized by the male as they are deposited. Young tadpoles have external gills for absorbing oxygen underwater, and internal gills as they grow bigger. The tail is slowly absorbed into the body. Hind legs grow first and then front legs.

29

Lungs develop and become ready for use as the gills disappear. The young adult frog is then ready to leave the water. Frogs can also absorb oxygen through their moist skins. Fully-grown frogs hibernate in the Winter in the mud at the bottom of lakes and ponds. A frog's tongue is hinged at the front of the mouth so that it can be flipped out to catch insects.

The largest frog in the world is the West African Goliath Frog. It can measure 14 inches from snout to rear vent, and 30 inches with its legs stretched out. One that weighed 7 lbs 13 ozs has been caught. The smallest, *Sminthillus limbatus,* is found in Cuba and is never more than half an inch in length.

The most virulent natural poison known is found in a frog called the Kokoi which lives in Colombia, South America. It has been used by the natives for poisoning their arrows. 0.0000004 of an ounce is enough to kill a man.

At the annual Calaveras County Jumping Frog Jubilee held in the United States on May 18, 1968, a swamp-bred frog called Corrosion leaped 36 times its own length to cover 18 feet $0\frac{1}{2}$ inch, a world record.

Folding instructions are on pages 37 & 38.

30

Tortoise

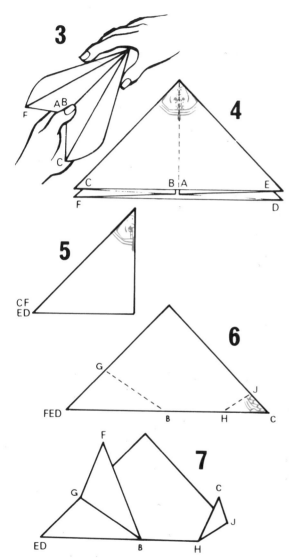

1. Lay the paper down with the eyes on top. Fold AB and then open out flat again.
2. Turn the paper over and fold CD. Open this out and do the same with EF. Open out flat again.
3. Take point B over to point A and hold them together in your left hand. Press the two sides together with your other hand.
4. This is how your Tortoise should look.
5. Fold the model in half and lay it on its side.
6. Turn the top flap back again.
7. Fold GB and JH.
8. Turn the next two flaps over.
9. Fold ML and AK.
10. Turn the last flap over and lay your Tortoise on his side.
11. Fold NO first to the left of the model and then to the right.
12. Do the same with QP.
13. Push the head back inside the Tortoise as far as NO will allow. The head will be inside out.
14. Pull the head out again as far as QP will allow.
15. Fold RS first to one side of the model and then to the other. Straighten this out.
16. Push point T back inside the nose as far as RS.
17. Fold the shell inwards on both sides at UV. This should only be a slight fold, not a sharp crease. Illustration shows Tortoise as seen from the back.

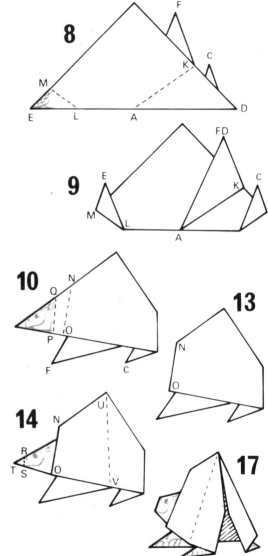

Otter

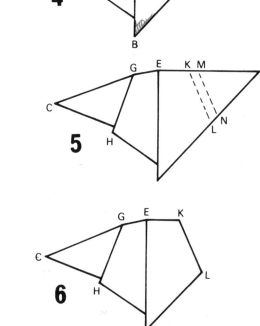

1

4

5

6

1. Fold AB and open out again. Fold CD.
2. Fold EF first to one side of the model and then to the other, then straighten this fold out again.
3. Do the same with GH, GJ, KL and MN. Straighten each one out before starting the next.
4. Push fold EF back inside the model as far as EB and EA will allow.
5. Push GJ back inside the model as far as fold GH will allow.
6. Push the tail inside the model as far as KL will allow.
7. Pull it out again as far as MN will allow.
8. Fold the whole model at PD, first to one side and then to the other. Straighten this fold out again.
9. Fold one foot up at OL.
10. Do the same with the foot on the other side.
11. Push OL up inside the model so that the feet show just below the body.
12. Fold QP first to one side of the model and then to the other. Straighten this out again and do the same with RS and RT.
13. Push RT inside the head as far as RS will allow. Do the same with point C and QP. Bend the feet outwards and pull the body apart a little way.

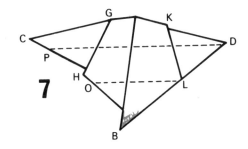

7

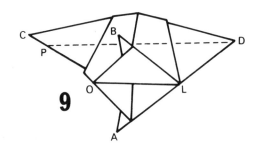

9

11

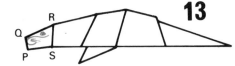

13

Pheasant

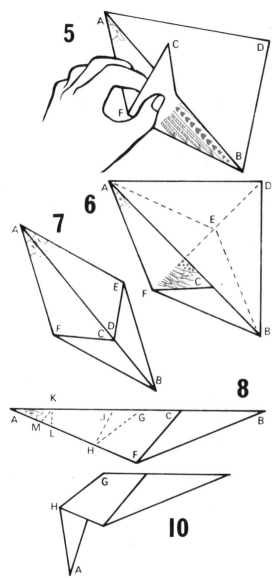

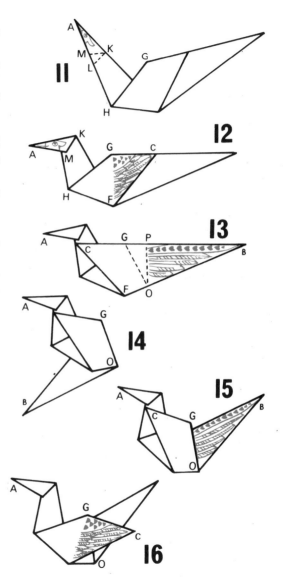

1. Lay the paper down with the eyes on top then fold AB. Open out flat again.
2. Turn the paper over and fold CD. Open out again.
3. Fold FB. Try not to crease the paper further than point F. Open out flat.
4. Now do the same with FA, EA and EB.
5. Lift point C and push edges AC and BC over to the fold AB, at the same time keep C standing up.
6. Fold the wing down flat so that C points towards B.
7. Repeat the last two stages with point D.
8. Fold the model in half so that there is a wing on each side.
9. Fold GH, JH, KL and KM. Make each fold first to one side of the model and then to the other. Straighten each fold out before starting the next one.
10. Push the neck down inside the model as far as GH will allow. The head should now be inside out.
11. Pull the head up again as far as JH will allow.
12. Push the head down as far as MK and LK will allow. Make sure that the head is outside the neck on both sides.
13. Fold the wings forward and make folds GO and PO first to one side of the body and then to the other, as you did with the neck.
14. Push the tail down inside the body as far as GO will allow. The tail is now inside out.
15. Pull the tail out again as far as PO will allow.
16. Fold the wings back again and the Pheasant is complete.

33

Snail

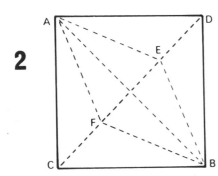

2

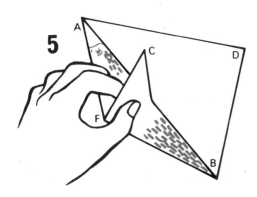

5

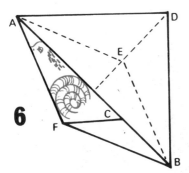

6

1. Lay the paper down with the shell on top and then fold **AB**. Open out flat again.

2. Turn the paper over and fold **CD**. Open out again.

3. Fold **FB**. Try not to crease the paper further than point F. Open out flat.

4. Now do the same with **FA, EA** and **EB**.

5. Lift point C and push edges AC and BC over to the fold AB, at the same time keep C standing up.

6. Fold C down so that it points towards **B**.

7. Repeat the last two stages with point **D**.

8. Fold the model in half along **AB** so that there is a flap on each side.

9. Fold GH, KJ, KL, ML, NO and PQ. Make each fold first to one side of the model and then to the other. Straighten each fold out before starting the next.

10. Push the neck inside the body as far as GH will allow. The head is now inside out.

Continued

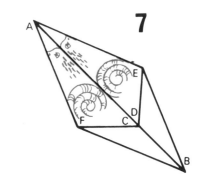

7

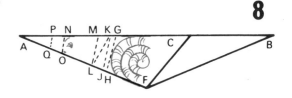

8

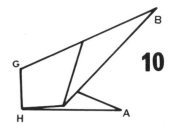

10

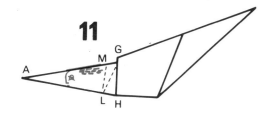

11

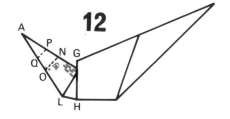

12

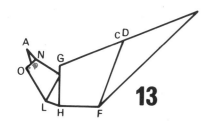

13

Snail continued

11. Pull the head forward again as far as KJ will allow.

12. Do the same with folds KL and ML.

13. Do the same again with NO and PQ.

14. Fold the two side flaps forward and fold RS from side to side, then straighten out.

15. Push the tail inside the body as far as TF will allow and pull it out again from RS.

16. Hold a side flap in each hand and push C inside D so that the two crosses are just covered.

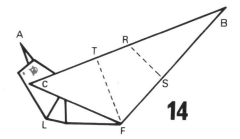

14

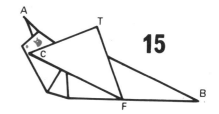

15

16

Hedgehog

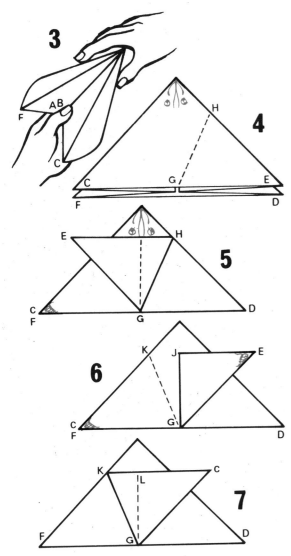

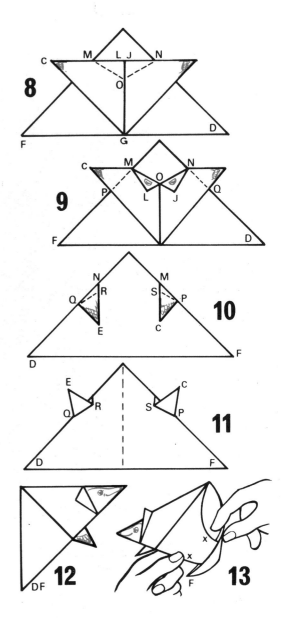

1. Lay the paper down with the eyes on top. Fold AB and then open out flat again.

2. Turn the paper over and fold CD. Open this out and do the same with EF. Open out flat again.

3. Take point B over to point A and hold them together in your left hand. Press the two sides together with your other hand.

4. This is how your Hedgehog should look.

5. Fold GH.

6. Fold JG.

7. Fold KG.

8. Fold LG.

9. Fold NO and MO.

10. Fold MP and NQ so that C and E are underneath the model. Now turn the model over.

11. Fold QR and SP.

12. Fold the model in half.

13. Push point F inside point D so that the two crosses are just covered.

Frog

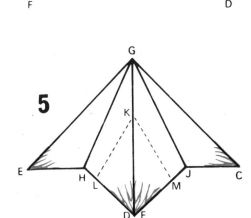

3

4

5

1. Lay the paper down with the eyes on top. Fold AB and then open out flat again.

2. Turn the paper over and fold CD. Open this out and do the same with EF. Open out flat again.

3. Take point B over to point A and hold them together in your left hand. Press the two sides together with your other hand.

4. This is how your Frog should look.

5. Turn the model over and fold GH and GJ.

6. Fold KL and KM. The back legs are now finished.

7. Fold one leg over on top of the other.

8. Fold NB.

9. Fold OB.

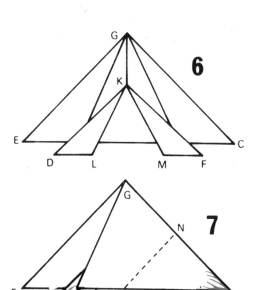

6

7

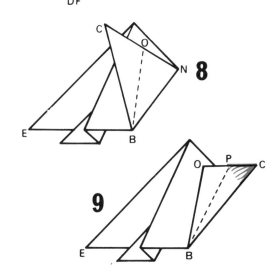

8

9

Continued

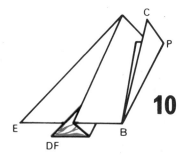

10

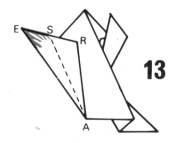

13

Frog continued

10. Fold PB.

11. Fold the two legs over to the other side.

12. Fold QA.

13. Fold RA.

14. Fold SA.

15. Fold one back leg over again. Pull the front legs slightly away from the body and stand the Frog on his feet.

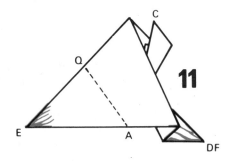

11

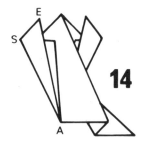

14

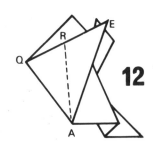

12

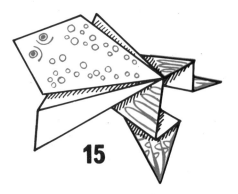

15